PETER RABBIT GIANT TREASURY

BY BEATRIX POTTER,
WITH HER ORIGINAL ILLUSTRATIONS

The Tale of Peter Rabbit
The Tailor of Gloucester • The Tale of Squirrel Nutkin
The Tale of Benjamin Bunny • The Tale of Two Bad Mice
The Tale of Mrs. Tiggy-winkle • The Pie and the Patty-Pan
The Tale of Mr. Jeremy Fisher

Edited and with an Introduction by Cary Wilkins

Derrydale Books• New York

CONTENTS

"The Tailor of Gloucester" and "The Pie and the Patty-Pan" have been edited for this edition.

This edition is published by Derrydale Books,
distributed by Crown Publishers, Inc.,
One Park Avenue, New York, New York 10016

Manufactured in the United States of America

Library of Congress Cataloging in Publication Data

Potter, Beatrix, 1866-1943.
   Peter Rabbit giant treasury.
   CONTENTS: The tale of Peter Rabbit.—The tailor of
Gloucester.—The tale of Squirrel Nutkin. [etc.]
   1. Children's stories, English. [1. Animals—
Fiction. 2. Short stories] I. Title.
PZ7.P85Be   1980   [E]   80-13368
ISBN 0-517-31687-0

s   r

INTRODUCTION

As with many writers of successful children's books, Beatrix Potter had a great rapport with children. Never having forgotten her own childhood delights, she knew what would interest and amuse her young readers. She kept her spirit of childlike wonder.

Her imaginative world of little animals and their adventures was the same one that fascinated her as a child. Born into a well-to-do family in London in 1866, her childhood was intensely lonely: little warmth from her parents and relatives and no friendship with other children, except her brother Bertram. But her isolation did not cause an unhealthy retreat into herself. On holidays in Scotland, she and Bertram escaped into a world of farms, woods, and fields. They collected plants, animals, and insects; unknown to their parents, they even brought home dead animals in order to draw and paint them.

This love of nature was coupled with a creative imagination to produce some of the most beloved stories in literature. But the stories are not sentimental ones of cute and precious little animals. They are lively tales of independent little creatures who have places to go and things to do.

Miss Potter, however, did not enjoy the independence her characters did. She was tied to her parents until she was forty-seven, when she married William Heelis. Even at that age, she had to contend with her parents' opposition to the marriage.

She did, however, possess the same toughness that her characters had—an acceptance of how things must be. During her years on Hill Top Farm, she wrote to a friend that, as a farmer, she could not be sentimental: she was resolved to have some hearthrugs made of lambskin. In her stories, mice are always on the lookout for cats and owls; rabbits must learn to outsmart irritable gardeners whose wives make excellent rabbit pies; and big fish are always ready to have little frogs for dinner. Beatrix Potter appreciated the beauties of nature while respecting its ruthlessness. This attitude makes her stories true to life and to the laws of nature, and is one reason why they have appealed to people for so many years.

Another reason for their continued popularity was given by Beatrix Potter herself: she attributed *Peter Rabbit's* success to the fact that it was originally written as a letter to a child. Her first three stories and other later ones began as illustrated letters to children. *Peter Rabbit* was the first, written on September 4, 1893, to Noël Moore, a child of Beatrix's former governess. Deciding to make it into a book several years later, Miss Potter had it privately printed, after no publisher would accept it. Recognizing its merits and success, Frederick Warne later agreed to publish it, and thus began a happy relationship lasting for many years and many books.

Eight of her delightful tales are reprinted here in chronological order. For models for the illustrations, Beatrix Potter drew her own pets and animal acquaintances. First there's brave Peter Rabbit striking out on his own to explore the garden of Mr. McGregor. Who can erase from memory the sight of little Peter rounding the corner of a cucumber frame and stopping dead in his tracks to confront a surprised Mr. McGregor? Then there's a delightful story with a fairy-tale quality about a tired old tailor and the mysterious appearance of a beautiful waistcoat—minus one buttonhole. In an unfortunate "tale of a tail," Squirrel Nutkin amuses us (but not Old Brown) with challenging riddles, whose answers are incorporated into the text. Peter reappears with his cousin Benjamin Bunny for a trip back to the garden. This time they're trapped until old Mr. Bunny saves the day. Those two bad mice, Tom Thumb and Hunca Munca, warm our hearts when we find out they're not so bad after all. But who can really blame them for getting upset about a ham made out of plaster, and fish that's glued to a plate? With all the running around these adventurous creatures do, it's no wonder their clothes get dirty. But they come out fresh as new when Mrs. Tiggy-winkle gets hold of them. In another tale, we see the complications that arise when Ribby, a cat, invites Duchess, a dog, to have mouse pie for tea. And more frogs should follow the example of Mr. Jeremy Fisher when they go fishing: always wear a mackintosh, because fish like to go frogging, but they don't like the taste of rubber.

In her later years as a sheep farmer and property owner, Mrs. William Heelis left Beatrix Potter behind. But she also left many wonderful stories and pictures, brimming with life and humor, which will always delight and amuse us.

CARY WILKINS

THE TALE OF

PETER RABBIT

ONCE upon a time there were four little Rabbits, and their names were—

Flopsy,
Mopsy,
Cotton-tail,
and Peter.

They lived with their Mother in a sand-bank, underneath the root of a very big fir-tree.

"Now, my dears," said old Mrs. Rabbit one morning, "you may go into the fields or down the lane, but don't go into Mr. McGregor's garden: your Father had an accident there; he was put in a pie by Mrs. McGregor."

"Now run along, and don't get into mischief. I am going out."

Then old Mrs. Rabbit took a basket and her umbrella, and went through the wood to the baker's. She bought a loaf of brown bread and five currant buns.

Flopsy, Mopsy, and Cotton-tail, who were good little bunnies, went down the lane to gather blackberries;

But Peter, who was very naughty, ran straight away to Mr. McGregor's garden, and squeezed under the gate!

First he ate some lettuces and some French beans; and then he ate some radishes;

And then, feeling rather sick, he went to look for some parsley.

But round the end of a cucumber frame, whom should he meet but Mr. McGregor!

Mr. McGregor was on his hands and knees planting out young cabbages, but he jumped up and ran after Peter, waving a rake and calling out, "Stop thief!"

Peter was most dreadfully frightened; he rushed all over the garden, for he had forgotten the way back to the gate.

He lost one of his shoes among the cabbages, and the other shoe amongst the potatoes.

After losing them, he ran on four legs and went faster, so that I think he might have got away altogether if he had not unfortunately run into a gooseberry net, and got caught by the large buttons on his jacket. It was a blue jacket with brass buttons, quite new.

Peter gave himself up for lost, and shed big tears; but his sobs were overheard by some friendly sparrows, who flew to him in great excitement, and implored him to exert himself.

Mr. McGregor came up with a sieve, which he intended to pop upon the top of Peter; but Peter wriggled out just in time, leaving his jacket behind him.

And rushed into the toolshed, and jumped into a can. It would have been a beautiful thing to hide in, if it had not had so much water in it.

Mr. McGregor was quite sure that Peter was somewhere in the tool-shed, perhaps hidden underneath a flower-pot. He began to turn them over carefully, looking under each.

Presently Peter sneezed—"Ker-tyschoo!" Mr. McGregor was after him in no time,

And tried to put his foot upon Peter, who jumped out of a window, upsetting three plants. The window was too small for Mr. McGregor, and he was tired of running after Peter. He went back to his work.

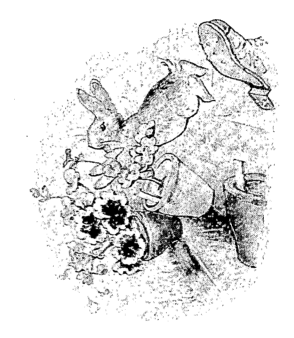

Peter sat down to rest; he was out of breath and trembling with fright, and he had not the least idea which way to go. Also he was very damp with sitting in that can.

After a time he began to wander about, going lippity—lippity—not very fast, and looking all around.

He found a door in a wall; but it was locked, and there was no room for a fat little rabbit to squeeze underneath.

An old mouse was running in and out over the stone doorstep, carrying peas and beans to her family in the wood. Peter asked her the way to the gate, but she had such a large pea in her mouth that she could not answer. She only shook her head at him. Peter began to cry.

Then he tried to find his way straight across the garden, but he became more and more puzzled. Presently, he came to a pond where Mr. McGregor filled his water-cans. A white cat was staring at some goldfish; she sat very, very still, but now and then the tip of her tail twitched as if it were alive. Peter thought it best to go away without speaking to her; he had heard about cats from his cousin, little Benjamin Bunny.

He went back towards the tool-shed, but suddenly, quite close to him, he heard the noise of a hoe—scr-r-ritch, scratch, scratch, scritch. Peter scuttered underneath the bushes. But presently, as nothing happened, he came out, and climbed upon a wheelbarrow, and peeped over. The first thing he saw was Mr. McGregor hoeing onions. His back was turned towards Peter, and beyond him was the gate!

Peter got down very quietly off the wheelbarrow, and started running as fast as he could go, along a straight walk behind some black-currant bushes.

Mr. McGregor caught sight of him at the corner, but Peter did not care. He slipped underneath the gate, and was safe at last in the wood outside the garden.

Mr. McGregor hung up the little jacket and the shoes for a scare-crow to frighten the blackbirds.

Peter never stopped running or looked behind him till he got home to the big fir-tree.

He was so tired that he flopped down upon the nice soft sand on the floor of the rabbit-hole, and shut his eyes. His mother was busy cooking; she wondered what he had done with his clothes. It was the second little jacket and pair of shoes that Peter had lost in a fortnight!

I am sorry to say that Peter was not very well during the evening.

His mother put him to bed, and made some camomile tea; and she gave a dose of it to Peter!

"One table-spoonful to be taken at bed-time."

But Flopsy, Mopsy, and Cotton-tail had bread and milk and blackberries, for supper.

THE END.

THE TAILOR OF GLOUCESTER

"I'll be at charges for a looking-glass;
And entertain a score or two of tailors."
Richard III

My Dear Freda:

Because you are fond of fairytales, and have been ill, I have made you a story all for yourself—a new one that nobody has read before.

And the queerest thing about it is—that I heard it in Gloucestershire, and that it is true—at least about the tailor, the waistcoat, and the

"No more twist!"

Christmas.

IN the time of swords and periwigs and full-skirted coats with flowered lappets—when gentlemen wore ruffles, and gold-laced waistcoats of paduasoy and taffeta—there lived a tailor in Gloucester.

He sat in the window of a little shop in Westgate Street, cross-legged on a table from morning till dark.

All day long while the light lasted he sewed and snippetted, piecing out his satin, and pompadour, and lutestring; stuffs had strange names, and were very expensive in the days of the Tailor of Gloucester.

But although he sewed fine silk for his neighbours, he himself was very, very poor. He cut his coats without waste; according to his embroidered cloth, they were very small ends and snippets that lay about upon the table—"Too narrow breadths for nought—except waistcoats for mice," said the tailor.

One bitter cold day near Christmastime the tailor began to make a coat (a coat of cherry-coloured corded silk embroidered with pansies and roses) and a cream-coloured satin waistcoat for the Mayor of Gloucester.

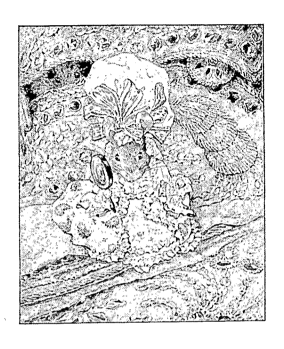

The tailor worked and worked, and he talked to himself: "No breadth at all, and cut on the cross; it is no breadth at all; tippets for mice and ribbons for mobs! for mice!" said the Tailor of Gloucester.

When the snow-flakes came down against the small leaded window-panes and shut out the light, the tailor had done his day's work; all the silk and satin lay cut out upon the table.

There were twelve pieces for the coat and four pieces for the waist-coat; and there were pocket-flaps and cuffs and buttons, all in order. For the lining of the coat there was fine yellow taffeta, and for the button-holes of the waistcoat there was cherry-coloured twist. And every-thing was ready to sew together in the morning, all measured and sufficient—except that there was wanting just one single skein of cherry-coloured twisted silk.

The tailor came out of his shop at dark. No one lived there at nights but little brown mice, and *they* ran in and out without any keys!

For behind the wooden wainscots of all the old houses in Gloucester, there are little mouse staircases and secret trap-doors; and the mice run from house to house through those long, narrow passages.

But the tailor came out of his shop and shuffled home through the snow. And although it was not a big house, the tailor was so poor he only rented the kitchen.

He lived alone with his cat; it was called Simpkin.

"Miaw?" said the cat when the tailor opened the door, "miaw?"

The tailor replied: "Simpkin, we shall make our fortune, but I am worn to a ravelling. Take this groat (which is our last fourpence), and, Simpkin, take a china pipkin, buy a penn'orth of bread, a penn'orth of milk, and a penn'orth of sausages. And oh, Simpkin, with the last penny of our fourpence buy me one penn'orth of cherry-coloured silk. But do not lose the last penny of the fourpence, Simpkin, or I am undone and worn to a thread-paper, for I have NO MORE TWIST."

Then Simpkin again said "Miaw!" and took the groat and the pipkin, and went out into the dark.

The tailor was very tired and beginning to be ill. He sat down by the hearth and talked to himself about that wonderful coat.

"I shall make my fortune—to be cut bias—the Mayor of Gloucester is to be married on Christmas Day in the morning, and he hath ordered a coat and an embroidered waistcoat—"

Then the tailor started; for suddenly, interrupting him, from the dresser at the other side of the kitchen came a number of little noises—

Tip tap, tip tap, tip tap tip!

"Now what can that be?" said the Tailor of Gloucester, jumping up from his chair. The tailor crossed the kitchen, and stood quite still beside the dresser, listening, and peering through his spectacles.

"This is very peculiar," said the Tailor of Gloucester, and he lifted up the tea-cup which was upside down.

Out stepped a little live lady mouse, and made a courtesy to the tailor! Then she hopped away down off the dresser, and under the wainscot.

The tailor sat down again by the fire, warming his poor cold hands. But all at once, from the dresser, there came other little noises—

Tip tap, tip tap, tip tap tip!

"This is passing extraordinary!" said the Tailor of Gloucester, and turned over another tea-cup, which was upside down.

Out stepped a little gentleman mouse, and made a bow to the tailor!

And out from under tea-cups and from under bowls and basins, stepped other and more little mice, who hopped away down off the dresser and under the wainscot.

The tailor sat down, close over the fire, lamenting: "One-and-twenty buttonholes of cherry-coloured silk! To be finished by noon of Saturday: and this is Tuesday evening. Was it right to let loose those mice, undoubtedly the property of Simpkin? Alack, I am undone, for I have no more twist!"

The little mice came out again and listened to the tailor; they took notice of the pattern of that wonderful coat. They whispered to one another about the taffeta lining and about little mouse tippets.

And then suddenly they all ran away together down the passage behind the wainscot, squeaking and calling to one another as they ran from house to house.

Not one mouse was left in the tailor's kitchen when Simpkin came back. He set down the pipkin of milk upon the dresser, and looked suspiciously at the tea-cups. He wanted his supper of little fat mouse!

"Simpkin," said the tailor, "where is my TWIST?"

But Simpkin hid a little parcel privately in the tea-pot, and spit and growled at the tailor; and if Simpkin had been able to talk, he would have asked: "Where is my MOUSE?"

"Alack, I am undone!" said the Tailor of Gloucester, and went sadly to bed.

All that night long Simpkin hunted and searched through the kitchen, peeping into cupboards and under the wainscot, and into the tea-pot where he had hidden that twist; but still he found never a mouse!

The poor old tailor was very ill with a fever, tossing and turning in his four-post bed; and still in his dreams he mumbled: "No more twist! no more twist!"

What should become of the cherry-coloured coat? Who should come to sew it, when the window was barred, and the door was fast locked?

Out-of-doors the market folks went trudging through the snow to buy their geese and turkeys, and to bake their Christmas pies; but there would be no Christmas dinner for Simpkin and the poor old tailor of Gloucester.

The tailor lay ill for three days and nights; and then it was Christmas Eve, and very late at night. And still Simpkin wanted his mice, and mewed as he stood beside the four-post bed.

But it is in the old story that all the beasts can talk in the night between Christmas Eve and Christmas Day in the morning (though there are very few folk that can hear them, or know what it is that they say).

When the Cathedral clock struck twelve there was an answer—like an echo of the chimes—and Simpkin heard it, and came out of the tailor's door, and wandered about in the snow.

From all the roofs and gables and old wooden houses in Gloucester came a thousand merry voices singing the old Christmas rhymes—all the old songs that ever I heard of, and some that I don't know, like Whittington's bells.

Under the wooden eaves the starlings and sparrows sang of Christmas pies; the jackdaws woke up in the Cathedral tower; and although it was the middle of the night the throstles and robins sang; the air was quite full of little twittering tunes.

But it was all rather provoking to poor hungry Simpkin.

From the tailor's shop in Westgate came a glow of light; and when Simpkin crept up to peep in at the window it was full of candles. There was a snippeting of scissors, and snappeting of thread; and little mouse voices sang loudly and gaily:

"Four-and-twenty tailors
Went to catch a snail,
The best man amongst them
Durst not touch her tail;
She put out her horns
Like a little kyloe cow.
Run, tailors, run! or she'll have you all e'en now!"

Then without a pause the little mouse voices went on again:

"Sieve my lady's oatmeal,
Grind my lady's flour,
Put it in a chestnut,
Let it stand an hour—"

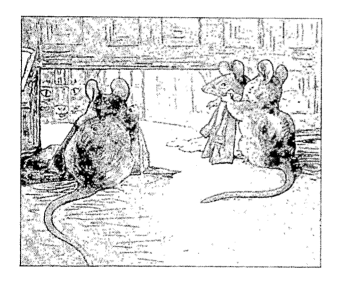

"Mew! Mew!" interrupted Simpkin, and he scratched at the door. But the key was under the tailor's pillow; he could not get in.

The little mice only laughed, and tried another tune—

"Three little mice sat down to spin,
Pussy passed by and she peeped in.
What are you at, my fine little men?
Making coats for gentlemen.
Shall I come in and cut off your threads?
Oh, no, Miss Pussy, you'd bite off our heads!"

"Mew! scratch! scratch!" scuffled Simpkin on the window-sill; while the little mice inside sprang to their feet, and all began to shout at once in little twittering voices: "No more twist! No more twist!" And they barred up the window-shutters and shut out Simpkin.

Simpkin came away from the shop and went home considering in his mind. He found the poor old tailor without fever, sleeping peacefully.

Then Simpkin went on tip-toe and took a little parcel of silk out of the tea-pot; and looked at it in the moonlight; and he felt quite ashamed of his badness compared with those good little mice!

When the tailor awoke in the morning, the first thing which he saw, upon the patchwork quilt, was a skein of cherry-coloured twisted silk, and beside his bed stood the repentant Simpkin!

The sun was shining on the snow when the tailor got up and dressed, and came out into the street with Simpkin running before him.

"Alack," said the tailor, "I have my twist; but no more strength—nor time—than will serve to make me one single buttonhole; for this is Christmas Day in the Morning! The Mayor of Gloucester shall be married by noon—and where is his cherry-coloured coat?"

He unlocked the door of the little shop in Westgate Street, and Simpkin ran in, like a cat that expects something.

But there was no one there! Not even one little brown mouse!

But upon the table—oh joy! the tailor gave a shout—there, where he had left plain cuttings of silk—there lay the most beautiful coat and embroidered satin waistcoat that ever were worn by a Mayor of Gloucester!

Everything was finished except just one single cherry-coloured buttonhole, and where that buttonhole was wanting there was pinned a scrap of paper with these words—in little teeny weeny writing—

NO MORE TWIST.

And from then began the luck of the Tailor of Gloucester; he grew quite stout, and he grew quite rich.

He made the most wonderful waistcoats for all the rich merchants of Gloucester, and for all the fine gentlemen of the country round.

Never were seen such ruffles, or such embroidered cuffs and lappets! But his buttonholes were the greatest triumph of it all.

The stitches of those buttonholes were so neat—*so* neat—I wonder how they could be stitched by an old man in spectacles, with crooked old fingers, and a tailor's thimble.

The stitches of those buttonholes were so small—*so* small—they looked as if they had been made by little mice!

THE END.

THE TALE OF

SQUIRREL NUTKIN

A STORY FOR NORAH

THIS is a Tale about a tail—a tail that belonged to a little red squirrel, and his name was Nutkin.

He had a brother called Twinkleberry, and a great many cousins: they lived in a wood at the edge of a lake.

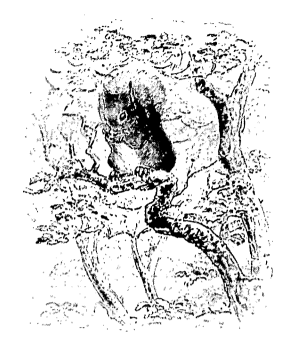

In the middle of the lake there is an island covered with trees and nut bushes; and amongst those trees stands a hollow oak-tree, which is the house of an owl who is called Old Brown.

One autumn when the nuts were ripe, and the leaves on the hazel bushes were golden and green—Nutkin and Twinkleberry and all the other little squirrels came out of the wood, and down to the edge of the lake.

They made little rafts out of twigs, and they paddled away over the water to Owl Island to gather nuts.

Each squirrel had a little sack and a large oar, and spread out his tail for a sail.

They also took with them an offering of three fat mice as a present for Old Brown, and put them down upon his door-step.

Then Twinkleberry and the other little squirrels each made a low bow, and said politely—

"Old Mr. Brown, will you favour us with permission to gather nuts upon your island?"

But Nutkin was excessively impertinent in his manners. He bobbed up and down like a little red *cherry*, singing—

"Riddle me, riddle me, rot-tot-tote!
A little wee man, in a red red coat!
A staff in his hand, and a stone in his
    throat;
If you'll tell me this riddle, I'll give you
    a groat."

Now this riddle is as old as the hills; Mr. Brown paid no attention whatever to Nutkin.

He shut his eyes obstinately and went to sleep.

The squirrels filled their little sacks with nuts, and sailed away home in the evening.

But next morning they all came back again to Owl Island; and Twinkleberry and the others brought a fine fat mole, and laid it on the stone in front of Old Brown's doorway, and said—

"Mr. Brown, will you favour us with your gracious permission to gather some more nuts?"

But Nutkin, who had no respect, began to dance up and down, tickling old Mr. Brown with a *nettle* and singing—

"Old Mr. B! Riddle-me-ree!
Hitty Pitty within the wall,
Hitty Pitty without the wall;
If you touch Hitty Pitty,
Hitty Pitty will bite you!"

Mr. Brown woke up suddenly and carried the mole into his house.

He shut the door in Nutkin's face. Presently a little thread of blue *smoke* from a wood fire came up from the top of the tree, and Nutkin peeped through the key-hole and sang—

"A house full, a hole full!
And you cannot gather a bowl-full!"

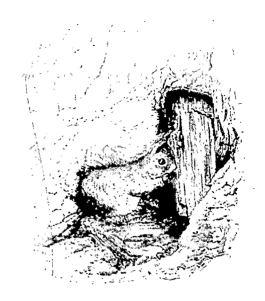

The squirrels searched for nuts all over the island and filled their little sacks.

But Nutkin gathered oak-apples— yellow and scarlet—and sat upon a beech-stump playing marbles, and watching the door of old Mr. Brown.

On the third day the squirrels got up very early and went fishing; they caught seven fat minnows as a present for Old Brown.

They paddled over the lake and landed under a crooked chestnut tree on Owl Island.

Twinkleberry and six other little squirrels each carried a fat minnow; but Nutkin, who had no nice manners, brought no present at all. He ran in front, singing—

"The man in the wilderness said to me,
  'How many strawberries grow in the sea?'
  I answered him as I thought good—
  'As many red herrings as grow in the wood.'"

But old Mr. Brown took no interest in riddles—not even when the answer was provided for him.

On the fourth day the squirrels brought a present of six fat beetles, which were as good as plums in *plum-pudding* for Old Brown. Each beetle was wrapped up carefully in a dock-leaf, fastened with a pine-needle-pin.

But Nutkin sang as rudely as ever—

"Old Mr. B! riddle-me-ree!
  Flour of England, fruit of Spain,
  Met together in a shower of rain;
  Put in a bag tied round with a string,
If you'll tell me this riddle, I'll give you a ring!"

Which was ridiculous of Nutkin, because he had not got any ring to give to Old Brown.

The other squirrels hunted up and down the nut bushes; but Nutkin gathered robin's pin-cushions off a briar bush, and stuck them full of pine-needle-pins.

On the fifth day the squirrels brought a present of wild honey; it was so sweet and sticky that they licked their fingers as they put it down upon the stone. They had stolen it out of a bumble *bees'* nest on the tippity top of the hill.

But Nutkin skipped up and down, singing—

"Hum-a-bum! buzz! buzz! Hum-a-bum buzz!
    As I went over Tipple-tine
    I met a flock of bonny swine;
Some yellow-nacked, some yellow backed!
    They were the very bonniest swine
    That e'er went over Tipple-tine."

Old Mr. Brown turned up his eyes in disgust at the impertinence of Nutkin.

But he ate up the honey!

The squirrels filled their little sacks with nuts.

But Nutkin sat upon a big flat rock, and played ninepins with a crab apple and green fir-cones.

On the sixth day, which was Saturday, the squirrels came again for the last time; they brought a new-laid *egg* in a little rush basket as a last parting present for Old Brown.

But Nutkin ran in front laughing, and shouting—

"Humpty Dumpty lies in the beck,
  With a white counterpane round his neck,
  Forty doctors and forty wrights,
  Cannot put Humpty Dumpty to rights!"

Now old Mr. Brown took an interest in eggs; he opened one eye and shut it again. But still he did not speak.

Nutkin became more and more impertinent—

"Old Mr. B! Old Mr. B!
Hickamore, Hackamore, on the King's
      kitchen door;
All the King's horses, and all the King's men,
Couldn't drive Hickamore, Hackamore,
Off the King's kitchen door!"

Nutkin danced up and down like a *sunbeam*; but still Old Brown said nothing at all.

Nutkin began again—

"Arthur O'Bower has broken his band,
He comes roaring up the land!
The King of Scots with all his power,
Cannot turn Arthur of the Bower!"

Nutkin made a whirring noise to sound like the *wind,* and he took a running jump right onto the head of Old Brown! . . .

Then all at once there was a flutterment and a scufflement and a loud "Squeak!"

The other squirrels scuttered away into the bushes.

When they came back very cautiously, peeping round the tree—there was Old Brown sitting on his door-step, quite still, with his eyes closed, as if nothing had happened.

* * * * * * *

But Nutkin was in his waistcoat pocket!

This looks like the end of the story; but it isn't.

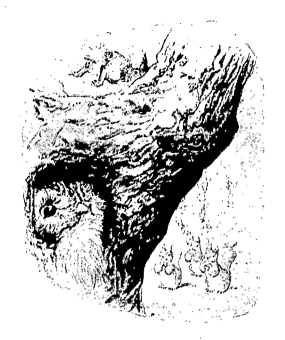

Old Brown carried Nutkin into his house, and held him up by the tail, intending to skin him; but Nutkin pulled so very hard that his tail broke in two, and he dashed up the staircase, and escaped out of the attic window.

And to this day, if you meet Nutkin up a tree and ask him a riddle, he will throw sticks at you, and stamp his feet and scold, and shout—

"Cuck-cuck-cuck-cur-r-r-cuck-k!"

THE END.

THE TALE OF
BENJAMIN BUNNY

FOR THE CHILDREN OF SAWREY
FROM
OLD MR. BUNNY

O NE morning a little rabbit sat on a bank.

He pricked his ears and listened to the trit-trot, trit-trot of a pony.

A gig was coming along the road; it was driven by Mr. McGregor, and beside him sat Mrs. McGregor in her best bonnet.

As soon as they had passed, little Benjamin Bunny slid down into the road, and set off—with a hop, skip, and a jump—to call upon his relations, who lived in the wood at the back of Mr. McGregor's garden.

That wood was full of rabbit holes; and in the neatest, sandiest hole of all lived Benjamin's aunt and his cousins—Flopsy, Mopsy, Cottontail, and Peter.

Old Mrs. Rabbit was a widow; she earned her living by knitting rabbit-wool mittens and muffatees (I once bought a pair at a bazaar). She also sold herbs, and rosemary tea, and rabbit-tobacco (which is what we call lavender).

Little Benjamin did not very much want to see his Aunt.

He came round the back of the fir-tree, and nearly tumbled upon the top of his Cousin Peter.

Peter was sitting by himself. He looked poorly, and was dressed in a red cotton pocket-handkerchief.

"Peter," said little Benjamin, in a whisper, "who has got your clothes?"

Peter replied, "The scarecrow in Mr. McGregor's garden," and described how he had been chased about the garden, and had dropped his shoes and coat.

Little Benjamin sat down beside his cousin and assured him that Mr. McGregor had gone out in a gig, and Mrs. McGregor also; and certainly for the day, because she was wearing her best bonnet.

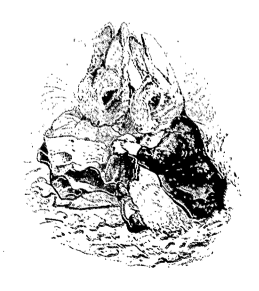

Peter said he hoped that it would rain.

At this point old Mrs. Rabbit's voice was heard inside the rabbit hole, calling: "Cotton-tail! Cotton-tail! fetch some more camomile!"

Peter said he thought he might feel better if he went for a walk.

They went away hand in hand, and got upon the flat top of the wall at the bottom of the wood. From here they looked down into Mr. McGregor's garden. Peter's coat and shoes were plainly to be seen upon the scarecrow, topped with an old tam-o'-shanter of Mr. McGregor's.

Little Benjamin said: "It spoils people's clothes to squeeze under a gate; the proper way to get in is to climb down a pear-tree."

Peter fell down head first; but it was of no consequence, as the bed below was newly raked and quite soft.

It had been sown with lettuces.

They left a great many odd little footmarks all over the bed, especially little Benjamin, who was wearing clogs.

Little Benjamin said that the first thing to be done was to get back Peter's clothes, in order that they might be able to use the pocket-handkerchief.

They took them off the scarecrow. There had been rain during the night; there was water in the shoes, and the coat was somewhat shrunk.

Benjamin tried on the tam-o'-shanter, but it was too big for him.

Then he suggested that they should fill the pocket-handkerchief with onions, as a little present for his Aunt.

Peter did not seem to be enjoying himself; he kept hearing noises.

Benjamin, on the contrary, was perfectly at home, and ate a lettuce leaf. He said that he was in the habit of coming to the garden with his father to get lettuces for their Sunday dinner.

(The name of little Benjamin's papa was old Mr. Benjamin Bunny.)

The lettuces certainly were very fine.

Peter did not eat anything; he said he should like to go home. Presently he dropped half the onions.

Little Benjamin said that it was not possible to get back up the pear-tree with a load of vegetables. He led the way boldly towards the other end of the garden. They went along a little walk on planks, under a sunny, red brick wall.

The mice sat on their doorsteps cracking cherry-stones; they winked at Peter Rabbit and little Benjamin Bunny.

Presently Peter let the pocket-handkerchief go again.

They got amongst flower-pots, and frames, and tubs. Peter heard noises worse than ever; his eyes were as big as lolly-pops!

He was a step or two in front of his cousin when he suddenly stopped.

This is what those little rabbits saw round that corner!

Little Benjamin took one look, and then, in half a minute less than no time, he hid himself and Peter and the onions underneath a large basket. . . .

The cat got up and stretched herself, and came and sniffed at the basket.

Perhaps she liked the smell of onions!

Anyway, she sat down upon the top of the basket.

She sat there for *five hours.*

* * * * * *

I cannot draw you a picture of Peter and Benjamin underneath the basket, because it was quite dark, and because the smell of onions was fearful; it made Peter Rabbit and little Benjamin cry.

The sun got round behind the wood, and it was quite late in the afternoon; but still the cat sat upon the basket.

At length there was a pitter-patter, pitter-patter, and some bits of mortar fell from the wall above.

The cat looked up and saw old Mr. Benjamin Bunny prancing along the top of the wall of the upper terrace.

He was smoking a pipe of rabbit-tobacco, and had a little switch in his hand.

He was looking for his son.

Old Mr. Bunny had no opinion whatever of cats. He took a tremendous jump off the top of the wall on to the top of the cat, and cuffed it off the basket, and kicked it into the greenhouse, scratching off a handful of fur.

The cat was too much surprised to scratch back.

When old Mr. Bunny had driven the cat into the greenhouse, he locked the door.

Then he came back to the basket and took out his son Benjamin by the ears, and whipped him with the little switch.

Then he took out his nephew Peter.

Then he took out the handkerchief of onions, and marched out of the garden.

When Mr. McGregor returned about half an hour later he observed several things which perplexed him.

It looked as though some person had been walking all over the garden in a pair of clogs—only the foot-marks were too ridiculously little!

Also he could not understand how the cat could have managed to shut herself up *inside* the greenhouse, locking the door upon the *outside*.

When Peter got home his mother forgave him, because she was so glad to see that he had found his shoes and coat. Cotton-tail and Peter folded up the pocket-handkerchief, and old Mrs. Rabbit strung up the onions and hung them from the kitchen ceiling, with the bunches of herbs and the rabbit-tobacco.

THE END.

THE TALE OF

TWO BAD MICE

FOR

W. M. L. W.

THE LITTLE GIRL

WHO HAD THE DOLL'S HOUSE

ONCE upon a time there was a very beautiful doll's-house; it was red brick with white windows, and it had real muslin curtains and a front door and a chimney.

It belonged to two Dolls called Lucinda and Jane; at least it belonged to Lucinda, but she never ordered meals.

Jane was the Cook; but she never did any cooking, because the dinner had been bought ready-made, in a box full of shavings.

There were two red lobsters and a ham, a fish, a pudding, and some pears and oranges.

They would not come off the plates, but they were extremely beautiful.

One morning Lucinda and Jane had gone out for a drive in the doll's perambulator. There was no one in the nursery, and it was very quiet. Presently there was a little scuffling, scratching noise in a corner near the fireplace, where there was a hole under the skirting-board.

Tom Thumb put out his head for a moment, and then popped it in again.

Tom Thumb was a mouse.

A minute afterwards, Hunca Munca, his wife, put her head out, too; and when she saw that there was no one in the nursery, she ventured out on the oilcloth under the coal-box.

The doll's-house stood at the other side of the fire-place. Tom Thumb and Hunca Munca went cautiously across the hearthrug. They pushed the front door—it was not fast.

Tom Thumb and Hunca Munca went upstairs and peeped into the dining-room. Then they squeaked with joy!

Such a lovely dinner was laid out upon the table! There were tin spoons, and lead knives and forks, and two dolly-chairs—all *so* convenient!

Tom Thumb set to work at once to carve the ham. It was a beautiful shiny yellow, streaked with red.

The knife crumpled up and hurt him; he put his finger in his mouth.

"It is not boiled enough; it is hard. You have a try, Hunca Munca."

Hunca Munca stood up in her chair, and chopped at the ham with another lead knife.

"It's as hard as the hams at the cheesemonger's," said Hunca Munca.

The ham broke off the plate with a jerk, and rolled under the table.

"Let it alone," said Tom Thumb; "give me some fish, Hunca Munca!"

Hunca Munca tried every tin spoon in turn; the fish was glued to the dish.

Then Tom Thumb lost his temper. He put the ham in the middle of the floor, and hit it with the tongs and with the shovel—bang, bang, smash, smash!

The ham flew all into pieces, for underneath the shiny paint it was made of nothing but plaster!

Then there was no end to the rage and disappointment of Tom Thumb and Hunca Munca. They broke up the pudding, the lobsters, the pears and the oranges.

As the fish would not come off the plate, they put it into the red-hot crinkly paper fire in the kitchen; but it would not burn either.

Tom Thumb went up the kitchen chimney and looked out at the top—there was no soot.

While Tom Thumb was up the chimney, Hunca Munca had another disappointment. She found some tiny canisters upon the dresser, labelled—

Rice—Coffee—Sago—but when she turned them upside down, there was nothing inside except red and blue beads.

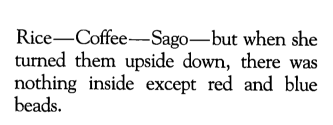

Then those mice set to work to do all the mischief they could—especially Tom Thumb! He took Jane's clothes out of the chest of drawers in her bedroom, and he threw them out of the top floor window.

But Hunca Munca had a frugal mind. After pulling half the feathers out of Lucinda's bolster, she remembered that she herself was in want of a feather bed.

With Tom Thumb's assistance she carried the bolster downstairs, and across the hearth-rug. It was difficult to squeeze the bolster into the mouse-hole; but they managed it somehow.

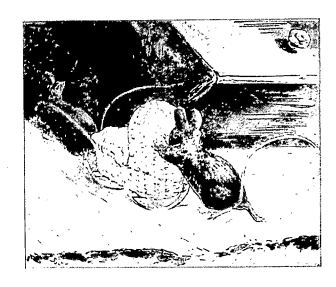

Then Hunca Munca went back and fetched a chair, a book-case, a bird-cage, and several small odds and ends. The book-case and the bird-cage refused to go into the mouse-hole.

Hunca Munca left them behind the coal-box, and went to fetch a cradle.

Hunca Munca was just returning with another chair, when suddenly there was a noise of talking outside upon the landing. The mice rushed back to their hole, and the dolls came into the nursery.

What a sight met the eyes of Jane and Lucinda! Lucinda sat upon the upset kitchen stove and stared; and Jane leant against the kitchen dresser and smiled—but neither of them made any remark.

The book-case and the bird-cage were rescued from under the coal-box—but Hunca Munca has got the cradle, and some of Lucinda's clothes.

She also has some useful pots and pans, and several other things.

The little girl that the doll's-house belonged to, said,—"I will get a doll dressed like a policeman!"

But the nurse said,—"I will set a mouse-trap!"

So that is the story of the two Bad Mice,—but they were not so very very naughty after all, because Tom Thumb paid for everything he broke.

He found a crooked sixpence under the hearth-rug; and upon Christmas Eve, he and Hunca Munca
stuffed it into one of the stockings of
Lucinda and Jane.

And very early every morning—
before anybody is awake—Hunca
Munca comes with her dust-pan and
her broom to sweep the Dollies'
house!

THE END.

THE TALE OF
MRS. TIGGY-WINKLE

FOR
THE REAL LITTLE LUCIE
OF NEWLANDS

ONCE upon a time there was a little girl called Lucie, who lived at a farm called Little-town. She was a good little girl—only she was always losing her pocket-handkerchiefs!

One day little Lucie came into the farm-yard crying—oh, she did cry so! "I've lost my pocket-handkin! Three handkins and a pinny! Have *you* seen them, Tabby Kitten?"

The Kitten went on washing her white paws; so Lucie asked a speckled hen—

"Sally Henny-penny, have *you* found three pocket-handkins?"

But the speckled hen ran into a barn, clucking—

"I go barefoot, barefoot, barefoot!"

And then Lucie asked Cock Robin sitting on a twig. Cock Robin looked

sideways at Lucie with his bright black eye, and he flew over a stile and away.

Lucie climbed upon the stile and looked up at the hill behind Little-town—a hill that goes up—up—into the clouds as though it had no top!

And a great way up the hillside she thought she saw some white things spread upon the grass.

Lucie scrambled up the hill as fast as her short legs would carry her; she ran along a steep path-way—up and up—until Little-town was right away down below—she could have dropped a pebble down the chimney!

Presently she came to a spring, bubbling out from the hillside.

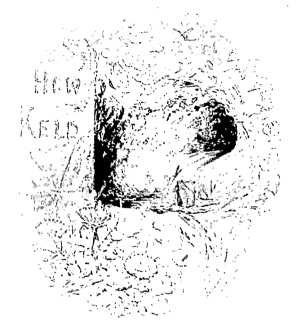

Some one had stood a tin can upon a stone to catch the water—but the water was already running over, for the can was no bigger than an egg-cup! And where the sand upon the path was wet—there were foot-marks of a *very* small person.

Lucie ran on, and on.

The path ended under a big rock. The grass was short and green, and there were clothes-props cut from bracken stems, with lines of plaited rushes, and a heap of tiny clothes pins—but no pocket-handkerchiefs!

But there was something else—a door! straight into the hill; and inside it some one was singing—

"Lily-white and clean, oh!
With little frills between, oh!
Smooth and hot—red rusty spot
Never here be seen, oh!"

Lucie knocked—once—twice, and interrupted the song. A little frightened voice called out "Who's that?"

Lucie opened the door: and what do you think there was inside the hill?—a nice clean kitchen with a flagged floor and wooden beams— just like any other farm kitchen. Only the ceiling was so low that Lucie's head nearly touched it; and the pots and pans were small, and so was everything there.

There was a nice hot singey smell; and at the table, with an iron in her hand, stood a very stout short person staring anxiously at Lucie.

Her print gown was tucked up, and she was wearing a large apron over

her striped petticoat. Her little black nose went sniffle, sniffle, snuffle, and her eyes went twinkle, twinkle; and underneath her cap—where Lucie had yellow curls—that little person had PRICKLES!

"Who are you?" said Lucie. "Have you seen my pocket-handkins?"

The little person made a bob-curtsey—"Oh yes, if you please'm; my name is Mrs. Tiggy-winkle; oh yes if you please'm, I'm an excellent clear-starcher!" And she took something out of a clothesbasket, and spread it on the ironing-blanket.

"What's that thing?" said Lucie—"that's not my pocket-handkin?"

"Oh no, if you please'm; that's a little scarlet waist-coat belonging to Cock Robin!"

And she ironed it and folded it, and put it on one side.

Then she took something else off a clothes-horse—"That isn't my pinny?" said Lucie.

"Oh no, if you please'm; that's a damask table-cloth belonging to Jenny Wren; look how it's stained with currant wine! It's very bad to wash!" said Mrs. Tiggy-winkle.

Mrs. Tiggy-winkle's nose went sniffle sniffle snuffle, and her eyes went twinkle twinkle; and she fetched another hot iron from the fire.

"There's one of my pocket-hand-kins!" cried Lucie—"and there's my pinny!"

Mrs. Tiggy-winkle ironed it, and goffered it, and shook out the frills.

"Oh that *is* lovely!" said Lucie.

"And what are those long yellow things with fingers like gloves?"

"Oh that's a pair of stockings be-longing to Sally Henny-penny—look how she's worn the heels out with scratching in the yard! She'll very soon go barefoot!" said Mrs. Tiggy-winkle.

"Why, there's another handker-sniff—but it isn't mine; it's red?"

"Oh no, if you please'm; that one belongs to old Mrs. Rabbit; and it *did* so smell of onions! I've had to wash it separately, I can't get out that smell."

"There's another one of mine," said Lucie.

"What are those funny little white things?"

"That's a pair of mittens belonging to Tabby Kitten; I only have to iron them; she washes them herself."

"There's my last pocket-handkin!" said Lucie.

"And what are you dipping into the basin of starch?"

"They're little dicky shirt-fronts belonging to Tom Titmouse—most terrible particular!" said Mrs. Tiggy-winkle. "Now I've finished my ironing; I'm going to air some clothes."

"What are these dear soft fluffy things?" said Lucie.

"Oh those are woolly coats belonging to the little lambs at Skelghyl."

"Will their jackets take off?" asked Lucie.

"Oh yes, if you please'm; look at the sheep-mark on the shoulder. And here's one marked for Gates-garth, and three that come from Little-town. They're *always* marked at washing!" said Mrs. Tiggy-winkle.

And she hung up all sorts and sizes of clothes—small brown coats of mice; and one velvety black mole-skin waist-coat; and a red tail-coat with no tail belonging to Squirrel Nutkin; and a very much shrunk blue jacket belonging to Peter Rabbit; and a petticoat, not marked, that had gone lost in the washing—and at last the basket was empty!

Then Mrs. Tiggy-winkle made tea—a cup for herself and a cup for Lucie. They sat before the fire on a bench and looked sideways at one another. Mrs. Tiggy-winkle's hand, holding the tea-cup, was very very brown, and very very wrinkly with the soap-suds; and all through her

gown and her cap, there were *hair-pins* sticking wrong end out; so that Lucie didn't like to sit too near her.

When they had finished tea, they tied up the clothes in bundles; and Lucie's pocket-handkerchiefs were folded up inside her clean pinny, and fastened with a silver safety-pin.

And then they made up the fire with turf, and came out and locked the door, and hid the key under the door-sill.

Then away down the hill trotted Lucie and Mrs. Tiggy-winkle with the bundles of clothes!

All the way down the path little animals came out of the fern to meet them; the very first that they met were Peter Rabbit and Benjamin Bunny!

And she gave them their nice clean clothes; and all the little animals and birds were so very much obliged to dear Mrs. Tiggy-winkle.

So that at the bottom of the hill when they came to the stile, there was nothing left to carry except Lucie's one little bundle.

Lucie scrambled up the stile with the bundle in her hand; and then she turned to say "Good-night," and to thank the washer-woman.—But what a *very* odd thing! Mrs. Tiggy-winkle had not waited either for thanks or for the washing bill!

She was running running running up the hill—and where was her white frilled cap? and her shawl? and her gown—and her petticoat?

And *how* small she had grown—and *how* brown—and covered with PRICKLES!

Why! Mrs. Tiggy-winkle was nothing but a HEDGEHOG!

* * * * * *

(Now some people say that little Lucie had been asleep upon the stile—but then how could she have found three clean pocket-handkins and a pinny, pinned with a silver safety-pin?

And besides—*I* have seen that door into the back of the hill called Cat Bells—and besides *I* am very well acquainted with dear Mrs. Tiggy-winkle!)

THE END.

THE PIE
AND
THE PATTY-PAN

Butter and milk from the farm.

Pussy-cat sits by the fire—how should she be fair?
In walks the little dog—says "Pussy are you there?
How do you do Mistress Pussy? Mistress Pussy, how do
    you do?"
"I thank you kindly, little dog, I fare as well as you!"

Old Rhyme.

ONCE upon a time there was a Pussy-cat called Ribby, who invited a little dog called Duchess to tea.

"Come in good time, my dear Duchess," said Ribby's letter, "and we will have something so very nice. I am baking it in a pie-dish—a pie-dish with a pink rim. You never tasted anything so good! And *you* shall eat it all! *I* will eat muffins, my dear Duchess!" wrote Ribby.

"I will come very punctually, my dear Ribby," wrote Duchess; and then at the end she added—"I hope it isn't mouse?"

The invitation.

And then she thought that did not look quite polite; so she scratched out "isn't mouse" and changed it to "I hope it will be fine," and she gave her letter to the postman.

But she thought a great deal about Ribby's pie, and she read Ribby's letter over and over again.

"I am dreadfully afraid it *will* be mouse!" said Duchess to herself—"I really couldn't, *couldn't* eat mouse pie. And I shall have to eat it, because it is a party. And *my* pie was going to be veal and ham. A pink and white pie-dish! and so is mine; just like Ribby's dishes; they were both bought at Tabitha Twitchit's."

Duchess went into her larder and took the pie off a shelf and looked at it.

"Oh what a good idea! Why shouldn't I rush along and put my pie into Ribby's oven when Ribby isn't there?"

Ribby in the meantime had received Duchess's answer, and as soon as she was sure that the little dog would come—she popped *her* pie into the oven. There were two ovens, one above the other; some other knobs and handles were only ornamental and not intended to open. Ribby put the pie into the lower oven; the door was very stiff.

"The top oven bakes too quickly," said Ribby to herself.

The pie made of mouse.

Ribby put on some coal and swept up the hearth. Then she went out with a can to the well, for water to fill up the kettle.

Then she began to set the room in order, for it was the sitting-room as well as the kitchen.

The veal and ham pie.

When Ribby had laid the table she went out down the field to the farm, to fetch milk and butter.

When she came back, she peeped into the bottom oven; the pie looked very comfortable.

Ribby put on her shawl and bonnet and went out again with a basket, to the village shop to buy a packet of tea, a pound of lump sugar, and a pot of marmalade.

And just at the same time, Duchess came out of *her* house, at the other end of the village.

Ribby met Duchess half-way down the street, also carrying a basket, covered with a cloth. They only bowed to one another; they did not speak, because they were going to have a party.

As soon as Duchess had got round the corner out of sight—she simply ran! Straight away to Ribby's house!

Ribby went into the shop and bought what she required, and came out, after a pleasant gossip with Cousin Tabitha Twitchit.

Ribby went on to Timothy Baker's and bought the muffins. Then she went home.

There seemed to be a sort of scuffling noise in the back passage, as she was coming in at the front door. But there was nobody there.

Where is the pie made of mouse?

Duchess in the meantime, had slipped out at the back door.

"It is a very odd thing that Ribby's pie was *not* in the oven when I put mine in! And I can't find it anywhere; I have looked all over the house. I put *my* pie into a nice hot oven at the top. I could not turn any of the other handles; I think that they are all shams," said Duchess, "but I wish I could have removed the pie made of mouse! I cannot think what she has done with it? I heard Ribby coming and I had to run out by the back door!"

Duchess went home and brushed her beautiful black coat; and then she picked a bunch of flowers in her garden as a present for Ribby; and passed the time until the clock struck four.

Ribby—having assured herself by careful search that there was really no one hiding in the cupboard or in the larder—went upstairs to change her dress.

She came downstairs again, and made the tea, and put the teapot on the hob. She peeped again into the *bottom* oven, the pie had become a lovely brown, and it was steaming hot.

She sat down before the fire to wait for the little dog. "I am glad I used the *bottom* oven," said Ribby, "the top one would certainly have been very much too hot."

Ready for the party.

Very punctually at four o'clock, Duchess started to go to the party.

At a quarter past four to the minute, there came a most genteel little tap-tappity. "Is Mrs. Ribston at home?" inquired Duchess in the porch.

"Come in! and how do you do, my dear Duchess?" cried Ribby. "I hope I see you well?"

"Quite well, I thank you, and how do *you* do, my dear Ribby?" said Duchess. "I've brought you some flowers; what a delicious smell of pie!"

"Oh, what lovely flowers! Yes, it is mouse and bacon!"

"I think it wants another five minutes," said Ribby. "Just a shade longer; I will pour out the tea, while we wait. Do you take sugar, my dear Duchess?"

Duchess in the porch.

"Oh yes, please! my dear Ribby; and may I have a lump upon my nose?"

"With pleasure, my dear Duchess."

Duchess sat up with the sugar on her nose and sniffed—

"How good that pie smells! I do love veal and ham—I mean to say mouse and bacon—"

She dropped the sugar in confusion, and had to go hunting under the tea-table, so did not see which oven Ribby opened in order to get out the pie.

Ribby set the pie upon the table; there was a very savoury smell.

Duchess came out from under the table-cloth munching sugar, and sat up on a chair.

"I will first cut the pie for you; I am going to have muffin and marmalade," said Ribby.

"I think"—(thought Duchess to herself)—"I *think* it would be wiser if I helped myself to pie; though Ribby did not seem to notice anything when she was cutting it. What very small fine pieces it has cooked into! I did not remember that I had minced it up so fine; I suppose this is a quicker oven than my own."

The pie-dish was emptying rapidly! Duchess had had four helps already, and was fumbling with the spoon.

"A little more bacon, my dear Duchess?" said Ribby.

"Thank you, my dear Ribby; I was only feeling for the patty-pan."

"The patty-pan? my dear Duchess?"

"The patty-pan that held up the pie-crust," said Duchess, blushing under her black coat.

"Oh, I didn't put one in, my dear Duchess," said Ribby; "I don't think that it is necessary in pies made of mouse."

Duchess fumbled with the spoon— "I can't find it!" she said anxiously.

"There isn't a patty-pan," said Ribby, looking perplexed.

"Yes, indeed, my dear Ribby; where can it have gone to?" said Duchess.

Duchess looked very much alarmed, and continued to scoop the inside of the pie-dish.

"I have only four patty-pans, and they are all in the cupboard."

Duchess set up a howl.

Where is the patty-pan?

"I shall die! I shall die! I have swallowed a patty-pan! Oh, my dear Ribby, I do feel so ill!"

"It is impossible, my dear Duchess; there was not a patty-pan."

"Yes there *was*, my dear Ribby, I am sure I have swallowed it!"

"Let me prop you up with a pillow, my dear Duchess; where do you think you feel it?"

"Oh I do feel so ill *all over* me, my dear Ribby."

"Shall I run for the doctor?"

"Oh yes, yes! fetch Dr. Maggotty, my dear Ribby: he is a Pie himself, he will certainly understand."

Ribby settled Duchess in an armchair before the fire, and went out and hurried to the village to look for the doctor.

She found him at the smithy.

Ribby explained that her guest had swallowed a patty-pan.

Dr. Maggotty hopped so fast that Ribby had to run. It was most conspicuous. All the village could see that Ribby was fetching the doctor.

But while Ribby had been hunting for the doctor—a curious thing had happened to Duchess, who had been left by herself, sitting before the fire, sighing and groaning and feeling very unhappy.

Dr. Maggotty's mixture.

"How *could* I have swallowed it! such a large thing as a patty-pan!"

She sat down again, and stared mournfully at the grate. The fire crackled and danced, and something sizz-z-zled!

Duchess started! She opened the door of the *top* oven;—out came a rich steamy flavour of veal and ham, and there stood a fine brown pie,—and through a hole in the top of the pie-crust there was a glimpse of a little tin patty-pan!

Duchess drew a long breath—

"Then I must have been eating Mouse! . . . No wonder I feel ill. . . . But perhaps I should feel worse if I had really swallowed a patty-pan!" Duchess reflected— "What a very awkward thing to have to explain to Ribby! I think I will put

my pie in the back-yard and say nothing about it. When I go home, I will run round and take it away." She put it outside the back-door, and sat down again by the fire, and shut her eyes; when Ribby arrived with the doctor, she seemed fast asleep.

"I am feeling very much better," said Duchess, waking up with a jump.

"I am truly glad to hear it! He has brought you a pill, my dear Duchess!"

"I think I should feel *quite* well if he only felt my pulse," said Duchess, backing away from the magpie, who sidled up with something in his beak.

"It is only a bread pill, you had much better take it; drink a little milk, my dear Duchess!"

"I am feeling very much better, my dear Ribby," said Duchess. "Do you not think that I had better go home before it gets dark?"

So there really *was* a patty-pan?

"Perhaps it might be wise, my dear Duchess."

Ribby and Duchess said good-bye affectionately, and Duchess started home. Half-way up the lane she stopped and looked back; Ribby had gone in and shut her door. Duchess slipped through the fence, and ran round to the back of Ribby's house, and peeped into the yard.

Upon the roof of the pig-stye sat Dr. Maggotty and three jackdaws. The jackdaws were eating piecrust, and the magpie was drinking gravy out of a patty-pan.

Duchess ran home feeling uncommonly silly!

When Ribby came out for a pailful of water to wash up the tea-things, she found a pink and white pie-dish lying smashed in the middle of the yard.

Ribby stared with amazement— "Did you ever see the like! so there really *was* a patty-pan? . . . But *my* patty-pans are all in the kitchen cupboard. Well I never did! . . . Next time I want to give a party—I will invite Cousin Tabitha Twitchit!"

THE END.

THE TALE OF

MR. JEREMY FISHER

FOR
STEPHANIE
FROM
COUSIN B.

ONCE upon a time there was a frog called Mr. Jeremy Fisher; he lived in a little damp house amongst the buttercups at the edge of a pond.

The water was all slippy-sloppy in the larder and in the back passage.

But Mr. Jeremy liked getting his feet wet; nobody ever scolded him, and he never caught a cold!

He was quite pleased when he looked out and saw large drops of rain, splashing in the pond—

"I will get some worms and go fishing and catch a dish of minnows for my dinner," said Mr. Jeremy Fisher. "If I catch more than five fish, I will invite my friends Mr. Alderman Ptolemy Tortoise and Sir Isaac Newton. The Alderman, however, eats salad."

Mr. Jeremy put on a mackintosh, and a pair of shiny galoshes; he took his rod and basket, and set off with enormous hops to the place where he kept his boat.

The boat was round and green, and very like the other lily-leaves. It was tied to a water-plant in the middle of the pond.

Mr. Jeremy took a reed pole, and pushed the boat out into open water. "I know a good place for minnows," said Mr. Jeremy Fisher.

Mr. Jeremy stuck his pole into the mud and fastened the boat to it.

Then he settled himself cross-legged and arranged his fishing tackle. He had the dearest little red float.

His rod was a tough stalk of grass, his line was a fine long white horse-hair, and he tied a little wriggling worm at the end.

The rain trickled down his back, and for nearly an hour he stared at the float.

"This is getting tiresome, I think I should like some lunch," said Mr. Jeremy Fisher.

He punted back again amongst the water-plants, and took some lunch out of his basket.

"I will eat a butterfly sandwich, and wait till the shower is over," said Mr. Jeremy Fisher.

A great big water-beetle came up underneath the lily leaf and tweaked the toe of one of his galoshes.

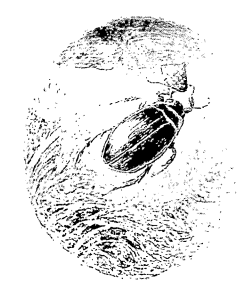

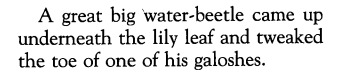

Mr. Jeremy crossed his legs up shorter, out of reach, and went on eating his sandwich.

Once or twice something moved about with a rustle and a splash amongst the rushes at the side of the pond.

"I trust that is not a rat," said Mr. Jeremy Fisher; "I think I had better get away from here."

Mr. Jeremy shoved the boat out again a little way, and dropped in the bait. There was a bite almost directly; the float gave a tremendous bobbit!

"A minnow! a minnow! I have him by the nose!" cried Mr. Jeremy Fisher, jerking up his rod.

But what a horrible surprise! Instead of a smooth fat minnow, Mr. Jeremy landed little Jack Sharp, the stickleback, covered with spines!

The stickleback floundered about the boat, pricking and snapping until he was quite out of breath. Then he jumped back into the water.

And a shoal of other little fishes put their heads out, and laughed at Mr. Jeremy Fisher.

And while Mr. Jeremy sat disconsolately on the edge of his boat—sucking his sore fingers and peering down into the water—a *much* worse thing happened; a really *frightful*

thing it would have been, if Mr. Jeremy had not been wearing a mackintosh!

A great big enormous trout came up—ker-pflop-p-p-p! with a splash—and it seized Mr. Jeremy with a snap, Ow! Ow! Ow!"—and then it turned and dived down to the bottom of the pond!

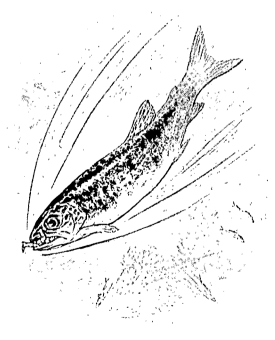

But the trout was so displeased with the taste of the mackintosh, that in less than half a minute it spat him out again; and the only thing it swallowed was Mr. Jeremy's galoshes.

Mr. Jeremy bounced up to the surface of the water, like a cork and the bubbles out of a soda water bottle; and he swam with all his might to the edge of the pond.

He scrambled out on the first bank he came to, and he hopped home across the meadow with his mackin-tosh all in tatters.

"What a mercy that was not a pike!" said Mr. Jeremy Fisher. "I have lost my rod and basket; but it does not much matter, for I am sure I should never have dared to go fishing again!"

He put some sticking plaster on his fingers, and his friends both came to dinner. He could not offer them fish, but he had something else in his larder.

Sir Isaac Newton wore his black and gold waistcoat.

And Mr. Alderman Ptolemy Tortoise brought a salad with him in a string bag.

And instead of a nice dish of minnows they had a roasted grasshopper with lady-bird sauce, which frogs consider a beautiful treat; but I think it must have been nasty!

THE END.